The Little Helpers

Tony and Beth Champine

Fulton Books
Meadville, PA

Published by Fulton Books 2024

ISBN 979-8-89221-497-1 (paperback)
ISBN 979-8-89427-307-5 (hardcover)
ISBN 979-8-89221-498-8 (digital)

Printed in the United States of America

Introduction

Growing up in Wisconsin, deer season is a part of many people's lives. The story you are about to read is true stories of different events that have happened over fifty-plus years of deer seasons. All these stories were put together for you to enjoy. Thank you for reading *The Little Helpers*.

Beth said, "Here it is, another deer-hunting season. For some reason, I feel it's going to be different."

Tony said, "I feel it too."

Beth kissed Tony, then put her arms around his neck and hugged him. Then she said, "Your beard grew very nice this year, a little grayer, but you kept it trimmed. Do you know who you remind me of?"

Tony said, "Let me guess, all the members of the group NSYNC."

Beth laughed and gave Tony's beard a little tug. "Right, Santa." Beth turned the TV on to catch the weather report, then said to Tony, "It's too bad our boys and your brothers couldn't make it up for the opening day this year."

Tony said, "That's all right. I'll just go through it alone today. They'll be here tomorrow. Maybe I'll have a good story to tell them."

Tony looked at some pictures that were displayed on the mantle above the fireplace. The pictures were of past hunting seasons. His favorite was the one of his father, who had passed away years earlier. In the photo, his father was wearing a red flannel coat with his gold pocket watch hanging out. He had an old-time Red Bombers hat and was wearing his heavy snow boots, with their trademark yellow laces.

His father was crouching down by a nice twelve-point buck, holding his rifle—the same rifle his father gave to him, and the one Tony uses to this day.

Beth was looking at the TV and said, "Looks like they posted blizzard warnings for later today." As she watched the TV, a special report came on. The TV announcer said, "Breaking News! An armed and very dangerous prisoner has escaped and is believed to be in the area. Please be on the lookout for him and use extreme caution. And again, repeating, our other top news, there is a severe blizzard heading our way."

Beth asked Tony, "What are your hunting plans for today?"

Tony answered, "I think I'll take that old logging road that goes west and hunt that lower ridge."

Beth laughed. "You're goofy. That's a long, long distance away!"

Tony said, "I've done that trek many times. I better get going now while it's early and before that storm gets here."

Beth said, "If you're going that far, I'm packing you all that leftover Halloween candy and extra protein bars I made."

Tony grumbled and said, "Beth, you're such a worrier."

Tony said, "Seeing that it is going to snow, I think I'll wear that old Red Bombers hat of my dad's over my skullcap liner. That will help keep me dryer and warmer." Tony picked up his rifle and stared at it a little while and said to Beth, "Maybe this year for Christmas, you could get me a new scope for my rifle."

Beth said, "I think I can do better than that!"

Tony thought to himself, *What is she talking about?* as he kissed Beth goodbye. He then patted their Samoyed dog, Frosty, on her head. Tony said to Frosty, "Take care of Beth and keep your eyes on the place while I'm gone." Frosty answered with an affirmative, "*Woof!*" Tony grabbed his backpack with all its gear and headed out the door.

As Tony made his way west to the old logging road, his thoughts drifted to past hunting seasons. He thought of all the people he had known and hunted with. Some of those just quit hunting, and others have passed on.

Tony thought to himself, *Maybe I'm getting too old for this.* He clicked on the radio he had clipped on his coat collar. The local radio station was playing Christmas music. Tony had been walking for a long time. It was late morning. Tony said to himself, "I'm close to where this road crosses with the north logging road. I think I'll take a rest there."

The snow began to fall…

When he got to the crossing, Tony couldn't believe his eyes. There was a young teacher with a group of little kids. The teacher said, "Hello, we are on a field trip. We're here collecting birch branches, boughs, pinecones, and other things to make wreaths and centerpieces for our school to sell at Christmas time."

Tony said with concern in his voice, "That sounds very nice, but you really should make your way back to your bus. You're a long way out, and there is a blizzard warning out."

The teacher said, "Oh, I'm sure we'll be all right." The kids gathered around Tony.

A little boy of African American descent yelled, "He's a hunter!"

"*Booo!*" they all yelled.

Then one little girl yelled, "He's a poopy head!"

"Yeah!" They all screamed.

8

A little boy of Middle-East descent said as he was shaking his finger at Tony, "You're a very, very bad man."

The children even got their yellow Lab that was with them to snarl at Tony.

The teacher tried to calm and settle the kids down. "I'm sorry," she said. But the insults just kept coming.

Tony said, "Oh, that's okay. You just be safe and get back to your bus like I asked."

Tony went on his way, heading deeper into the woods. He could still hear some insults and felt a few snowballs hitting him in his back. One snowball made its way to the back of his neck. Tony whispered to himself, "Good shot, kid. You kids remind me of some other knuckleheads I know."

At the same time, somewhere else, there was a devilish-looking man walking down a country road. He had just escaped prison. He was as evil as evil could get. He was ugly as ugly could get. On his mind was finding a way to steal a vehicle, get supplies, and flee the area. He was determined to do this anyway, and at any cost.

It was around midday, and Tony thought he better head back toward home because the snow had started falling. As he turned around, no further than fifty yards away, stood a huge twelve-point buck. Tony put the rifle on his shoulder and rested his arm and rifle on a tree limb to help take aim. He had the magnificent buck in the crosshairs of the sights. Gently, he put his finger on the trigger. Ready to squeeze off a sure shot. Tony thought, *I got you*, then Tony lowered the rifle. Tony whispered to himself, "I can't do it. I just can't bring myself to do it anymore, and somehow Beth knew it."

Slowly, the deer looked away, then looked back at Tony, flicked its tail, and walked away. The snow was falling hard, the blizzard was here early, and it had begun.

A short time later, Tony heard some commotion. It was that teacher with her group of kids. The teacher was in a panic. She was shaking and said, "Sir, we're lost. I don't know what to do. WE'RE LOST!"

Tony said, "Take it easy. I'll help you out, but we do have to get moving."

The teacher said, "Come on, children, we are going with this man. He's going to help us. Not one child moved." They all took a step back, even the dog that was with them backed up. The teacher said, "I think they are afraid of you."

Tony thought, *I need to think fast. I must win these kids over so I can help them.* Tony said to the children, "I need you guys to help me. I need your teacher and you to be my little helpers. Let me tell you a story." The children, with their teacher, gathered around Tony. The yellow lab sat next to the kids, still with a little growl coming from underneath its breath. Tony started his story.

"I'm really out here to find turkeys. My wife, Beth, and I want to invite them over to celebrate the holidays." Tony, sensing they were afraid of his rifle, said, "The only way to do it is to try to catch them first. This is a special magic rifle. You see, when I fire it, a magic net flies out to catch the turkeys." Tony looked at the children, gave them a sad frown, and said, "I've never caught one yet. I'll keep trying. Did you guys see any turkeys today?"

The kids answered, "Nooo."

Tony said, "Oh, I bet you did but didn't know it. They are very sneaky and tricky. They hide behind fallen trees and peek at you. They look just like sticks behind fallen trees. When I see one of those sticks, I know it's one of those sneaky turkeys peeking at me. I'll circle around the log and just like that, *poof*! They're gone. Then I hear that gobble, gobble, gobble, that's them laughing at me." The children, feeling calm and better, laughed at the story.

Tony said, "Now, will you be my little helpers? We'll go home and get some food to feed them. Beth and I feed them all the time. Maybe we will catch some turkeys, and we can all have a big party together!"

The excited kids yelled "OKAY!"

Tony said, "I'm calling you my Little Helpers."

The teacher said, "Let's go, children. We need to hurry. The blizzard is here."

Just then, a gobble, gobble, gobble was heard. The gray snowy day was rapidly turning into the dark of night. They would only have the reflection off the snow to help them see.

Tony took out his cell phone and called Beth. Tony said, "Beth, you are not going to believe this. I'm with a group of lost kids and their teacher." *Crackle...crackle...* the phone went.

Beth said, "You must hurry. The blizzard is moving in faster than was predicted." *Crackle…crackle* again went the phone. Beth said, "We're going to lose connection with this storm. I'll do what I can to…" *Crack, click, buzz,* then nothing—the connection was gone. Then a whimper and whine were heard from Frosty. Beth said to Frosty, "It will be all right. How about I let you out to play?"

Frosty loved the cold and snow, so off she went. She climbed on top of her favorite snowbank. She then laid down on top of the snowbank and stared off into the west as if she was looking for Tony and the lost group of kids.

As they walked, the snow was falling and getting deeper and deeper. The children were starting to struggle as they walked. To keep the children's minds off the long walk that was still ahead of them, Tony said to the children, "If you're going to be my little helpers, I need to give you little helpers names." As they walked, Tony went down the line of children and asked them their names and got to know a little bit about each one. After some thought, Tony said, "Let's stop and take a little rest break. I'll give you the nicknames I thought of for each of you." The kids were eager and excited to hear their new nicknames. A few were so excited they were holding their hands and jumping up and down.

Tony began to give the kids their new nicknames. To the European boy, he said, "Randy, you are Rudolf." To the Chinese boy, he called, "Donald, you are Donnor." To the African American boy, he said, "Amari, you are Dasher." To the African American girl, he said, "Connie, you are Vixen." To the Middle Eastern boy, he said, "Rashad, you are Blitzen." To the White girl, Tony continued, "Vickie, you are Cupid." To the other White girl, he said, "Virginia, you are Comet." And finally, to the two little Asian twin girls, he said, "Leah, you are Prancer, and Deanna, you are Dancer."

The kids asked, "What about Samantha, our dog?"

Tony said, "That's easy. She'll be Olive."

The kids yelled, "Olive! Why Olive?"

Tony said, "True story, didn't you know Olive was Santa's dog?" Look it up if you don't believe me. Olive was also one of Santa's little helpers." Tony looked at the teacher, "What is your name?"

She said, "I'm Mary."

Tony said, "That's perfect."

Tony tried calling Beth again on the cell phone. No luck, just buzzing. Thinking of the old TV western, Rawhide, he chuckled and said, "Okay, Little Helpers, let's head them up and move them out."

Tony gave his radio to the twins, Prancer and Dancer. He hoped this would help distract the kids and help keep their minds off the weather and the long hard walk. Tony said, "When a Christmas carol comes on, you little helpers sing along."

That idea lasted for a while. Then the kids said, "We're getting tired and bored."

Then Tony remembered the Halloween candy Beth had packed away. Tony thought, *Way to go Beth*.

Tony said, "Little Helpers, its snack time."

The kids screamed, "Hooray!" and jumped around.

He handed the huge bag of candy to Mary, and she passed it out to everyone. Tony reached into his pocket for a slab of jerky. Tony said, "Come here, Olive." Tony broke it up into pieces, and Olive gently ate it up. Tony petted Olive and said, "Now that we're friends, I know I can count on you to help me get these kids home safe."

The group didn't know what's lurking back in the woods. Not far away, there were four sets of eyes watching and staring at them. They were snarling, and drool was dripping from their fangs.

With the kids now feeling a little energized, Tony thought, *I must come up with a way to keep moving and cover more ground and to keep these kids warm.* Tony said, "Okay, Little Helpers, we are going to race. See that huge tree way, way over there? That will be the finish line. I'll have a prize for the winner. Ready? Set. Go!"

As they ran, the kids laughed and threw snow at each other. Olive even tackled some of the kids in the deep snow. At the finish line, Dasher jumped up and down. "I won! I won!" he screamed. "They don't call me Dasher for nothing." Tony took off his dad's bomber hat. He gave it a look and put it on Dasher's head. Dasher said, "Wow! Thanks. This hat is really, really nice and warm. I'm going to hang on to this forever." Everyone shared a laugh. Then they heard *gobble, gobble, gobble*.

Comet said, "That sounds like one of those turkeys we're looking for."

27

The kids said, "We don't want to run anymore. It's too hard. The snow is too deep, and we're getting tired."

Tony said, "Yes, I agree."

As they continued to walk and dredge their way slowly through the deep snow, Comet said to Tony, "Hey, Nick, we have a question to ask you."

Tony said, "Nick? Why did call me Nick?"

Comet said, "Well, you got to name us, so we get to name you."

The kids all started jumping up and down yelling, "Jolly Ol' St. Nick!"

Tony said, "Okay, okay, fair enough. Go ahead and ask Jolly Ol' St. Nick your question."

Comet asked, "We want to know why you didn't shoot that deer before?"

Tony was stunned, and his face went pale.

Mary said, "Just before you found us, we saw you from the ridge. We saw you take aim with a sure shot. Then saw you lower your rifle and not shoot."

Tony said, "I'll try to explain it to the kids." He gathered them around.

Tony said to the kids, "You guys know I'm out here to catch turkeys. I sure do need help doing that. So when I saw that deer, I thought maybe I could catch him to help me. Then I would explain to him why I needed his help to catch those sneaky turkeys. Then I heard you guys, so I thought instead I could ask you guys. I could ask you to be my little helpers. So I didn't need his help and he went home to be with his family."

The kids jumped up and down again and cheered, "We're glad we are your little helpers!" Tony looked over at Mary and gave her a wink and smile. Mary smiled back, and in her heart, she knew the truth why Tony did not shoot. Then came that *gobble, gobble, gobble*. Tony, with a silly voice, said, "There's that blasted noise again."

The kids all giggled and laughed, then said, "Nick, we're your little helpers. We'll help you catch them!"

It was dark now, and the blizzard was getting worse. Only the reflection of the snow would help them see a little. The kids said, "Nick, we are tired, hungry, and cold." Tony took off his backpack and coat and emptied both. He laid everything out to see what he all had. He gave Mary all the food to pass out to the kids. The food consisted of the rest of the Halloween candy, jerky, sausage, cheese, and protein bars that Beth made.

Comet and Cupid said, "These protein bars are so good. They're making us feel better. We would like Beth's recipes!"

Rudy said, "You really came prepared, Nick."

Donnor said, "Look at all this stuff."

Tony smiled at them and said, "Just remember this. Always be prepared when you venture out. You'll never know when you need it. It could save you, or someone else." Tony had a turkey sandwich with him. He didn't know how the kids would feel about the sandwich being turkey. Tony whispered to Olive, "Olive, come here." Tony fed Olive the sandwich and gave her the rest of the water he had. Everyone felt refreshed and energized.

Tony thought to himself, *It is dark and still snowing hard. It's time now to make one big push to get home.* He looked through the things he had with him. Tony yelled, "Hey, Randy!"

Randy yelled back, "I'm Rudy, remember?"

Tony said, "Okay, okay, Rudy, take the red flashlight because Donnor and you are going to lead."

Rudy—playing with the light, clicking it on and off by his nose—said, "Hey, I am Rudolph!"

Tony then gave Donnor his watch, which lit up and had a built-in compass. Tony showed Donnor a mark on the compass and told him to follow it in that direction. Tony said, "Pretend that's the North Pole, and it's our home."

Donnor then saluted Tony, smiled, and said, "Yes, sir!"

Tony saluted back. Tony grabbed the rope harness from his backpack. He tied it to Rudy, Donnor and Dasher at the front. Tony said to them, "You helpers are the leaders. You guys will be like snowplows and will be clearing a path for us."

Tony took Vixen next. Tony made a loop in the rope and put Vixen's hand in it. Tony took off his scarf and wrapped it around her neck. Tony said, "That should keep the snow out and keep you warm".

Vixen said, "I'm already getting warmer. Thanks!"

Tony said to Blitzen, "You're up next." Tony gave Blitzen his small first-aid kit, which had a couple of lighters in it.

Blitzen asked, "What's this for?"

Tony chuckled and said, "If the time comes, I want you to start the biggest fire you can, so big that Santa himself will see it from the North Pole."

Blitzen said, "Oh, Nick, you're funny." Then Tony put Comet and Cupid at the back of the line. Tony said, "Remember, you two are in charge of the radio. Keep those Christmas carols playing." Tony then gave them each a set of hand warmers. He then turned to Mary, "Here, put on this hoodie, you'll need it. In the pocket is my cell phone, keep calling and try to reach Beth, or anybody you can." Tony looked at the little twins and put an extra pair of mittens on each of them. "It's a good thing I had an extra pair," he told them. Just then, Rudy yelled back, "Nick, it's a good thing you came so prepared!"

"Like I told you before, I always do!" Tony replied.

The children looked at Tony, and he looked at the kids. Tony could feel they all were thinking something but couldn't tell what.

He turned to Mary. "The twins are too small and tired to go much further. I'm going to carry them on my shoulders. But to do that, I need to leave my rifle behind."

Mary gave out a sad, "*Nooo*, you can't do that."

Then Prancer and Dancer, with tears welling up their eyes, asked, "Nick, are we going to die out here?"

Tony said, "No way! I bet all of you will live into your nineties. Besides, you guys have important things in your lives you must do yet."

Now reassured, the girls smiled and said, "Oh, Nick, we would like you to see that."

Tony laid his rifle under a small blue spruce tree, with little hopes of finding it again. The kids sadly watched. Tony said to them, "Hey, just remember, it is a magic rifle. I'll see it again."

Tony rubbed his hands and chuckled. Then he said, "Okay now, on Dasher, on Prancer, on Comet, on Cupid…"

The kids laughed and yelled, "We get it, Nick!"

As they started on their final push home, there was that *gobble, gobble, gobble*.

The kids said, "Those turkeys are still teasing you, Nick."

Not far away, the wolf pack was watching. They had a plan of their own. The pack ran ahead of the group to prepare an ambush.

At the same time, the evil convict had thoughts of his own. His plan was to steal a vehicle and get the supplies he needed. He was going to escape once and for all, and he was going to do it at any cost.

Minutes after the group set off, a figure, who had been following Tony and the children, walked up to the rifle Tony had left behind. Picking it up, he brought it to his shoulder. He looked down the rifle scope. "This is nice, very nice," he said to himself. Taking aim at a tree limb, he pulled the trigger. The trigger clicked. "Very, very nice," he repeated.

Back at home, Beth was very worried. As night had come and the blizzard was getting worse, she still couldn't contact Tony. *I need to do something*, she thought to herself. She made her way to the garage and yelled for Frosty. "Frosty! Where are you? I know you love this weather, but it's no time to play." Frosty didn't come, which was odd. Beth had no time to look for her now.

She grabbed a set of chains from the shelf and strapped them on the tires of their four-wheel-drive truck before climbing in. As she went down the road, Beth sized up a huge pile of snow left behind by the snowplows. After staring at it for a while, she said, "Here we go!" Shifting the truck into four-wheel drive, she slammed the accelerator to the floor. Heading for the snow pile at a high rate of speed, Beth hit it at full force. Beth yelled at the truck, "CLIMB, BABY, CLIMB! COME ON. YOU CAN DO IT! CLIMB! DIG IN! DIG IN!" The truck tires just spun. She yelled again, "COME ON! CLIMB! DIG IN!" The truck motor started to whine and smoke. Beth yelled louder and harder, "CLIMB! DIG IN!" This time, the truck listened as the tires gripped and dug into the snow. The truck started to climb that giant pile of snow.

"COME ON, BABY! THAT'S IT, CLIMB!" The truck climbed into an almost vertical position before coming to a stop near the top. Knowing the truck wasn't going any higher, Beth shut the motor off and patted the dashboard. "I knew you could do it," she sighed to herself. Before climbing out of the truck, Beth turned the headlights on high. A bright beam of light shot into the night sky, piercing the darkness and illuminating the falling snow. As Beth walked back to the house, she again called for Frosty. With no answer, she looked back at the truck and said, "Lord, help us, and thank you, Jesus."

With only the reflection of the snow to help them see, the group continued making their way through the woods. Lost in thought, Tony started thinking, *We sure could use…* His thoughts came to a sudden stop. There it was, in the sky! A bright beam lighting up the dark snow-filled sky! The kids looked at the light as their jaws all dropped. Mary put her hands up to her face and said, "Oh holy star of Bethlehem!"

Unfortunately, the escaped convict who was in the area also saw the light. With an evil grin, he said, "Jackpot, my ticket out of here." He hurried toward the light, thinking everything he needed should be there.

Tony yelled to Rudy and Donner, "Head toward that light! It shouldn't be long now! We are almost home, Little Helpers!"

The kids were so excited that the slow pace they were going turned into a sprint. They started shouting all the things they were looking forward to when they got to Beth and Tony's home.

Comet and Cupid said, "We're going to get some more protein bars!"

Another shouted, "Us too! And a big glass of hot chocolate! And sit by that warm fireplace."

"I'm going to…"

The kids all stopped in their tracks. Putting the twins down, Tony walked to the front of the line by Rudy and Donnor. Staring ahead, he saw it. There, waiting, was the wolf pack. The wolves stared at the group with hunger in their eyes. They were growling, teeth showing and drool dripping from their jaws, waiting to attack.

Instinctively, Tony reached for the rifle on his shoulder. An ache went through his heart as he found it absent, remembering he had left it behind. Instead, he reached for his knife, and as he did, Olive took off toward the wolves.

Mary and Tony rushed the kids around the fight to safety. Then, with his knife in one hand, he reached for a stick with the other. Tony rushed back to help Olive. Suddenly, a white flash zoomed like a bolt of lightning past the group of kids. It was Frosty, darting in to help. There was growling, yelling, yelping, and screaming. Then silence. The kids strained their eyes to see in the darkness as they all wondered what happened. Then, like a light switch, the snow stopped. The clouds were gone. The sky was completely clear. The stars were out and brighter than ever. The northern lights appeared across the entire sky, beautiful and bright as ever.

"Look!" one of the children yelled. Emerging from the darkness as they walked toward the group was Olive and Frosty, followed by Tony. Looking down at the brave dogs with pride, Tony praised them. "We sure taught them a lesson, right girls?" The kids threw off the rope that held them together as they struggled through the deep snow and tackled the trio of heroes. Throughout the woods, there could be heard sounds of cheering and shouts of praise as the children passed out hugs. Tony looked at Mary and said, "They don't think I'm so bad after all."

Mary smiled as she replied, "I don't think they ever really did."

With the weather clearing, the cell phone started working again. "I made a couple of phone calls, including our bus driver, Gabe. He is on his way."

Tony said, "That's great. Let's go home."

As they approached Tony's home, Beth, who had heard the commotion, ran down the driveway to greet the group. There was much excitement and joy.

Back at the truck, the convict was rubbing his hands along the side of the truck. He looked at the group reunited at the home. He thought, *All I have to do is get rid of these people. That will be no problem. No evidence and no witnesses. I'll get inside that house, take what I want, get in this truck, and I'm home free, baby.* Just then, the convict felt a tap on his shoulder. As he turned around, he heard, "Merry Christmas," then "Good night." All he saw was a butt plate of a rifle heading toward his face, followed by darkness.

Beth turned around and saw coming up the road a snowplow pushing mountains of snow out of the way. The plow was being followed by an old school bus and a police car, all with lights flashing. *What is that bluish-white glow coming from inside that snowplow and bus?* she thought to herself. The bus stopped at the end of the driveway.

Out stepped a huge man dressed in a white parka and snow pants. "Gabe!" the kids yelled as they ran at the man, jumping into his arms as they hugged him. The police got out of their car. They walked over to the truck. There sat the convict with a gag over his mouth and tied up with yellow boots laces. An officer said, "Well, there you are. We've been looking for you." Another officer helped pick up the convict and put him in the police car. The sergeant looked up the driveway and yelled to Beth and Tony, "Thanks for the call, and thanks for nabbing this guy. I'm sure the community will sleep well tonight!"

Confused, Beth said, "Nabbing this guy? Who is that guy?"

Tony, equally confused, said, "Call? What call?"

A few feet away, Gabe said to Mary, "Looks like they got your call," as they shared a laugh with each other.

Beth said to everyone, "Let's go in the house and warm up, and we will have something to eat."

Tony said, "You guys go on in. I'll be right there. I have something I need to do first."

Tony went into the garage and got a couple of large buckets. He filled them to the brim with feed and seed. He went around the yard and spread the feed and seed all around. He looked at the northern lights and thoughts of thanks went through his mind.

As Tony entered the house, everyone was having a good time. The kids were surrounding the fireplace and eating snacks Beth had made earlier. Vickie and Virginia were asking Beth for her recipes. Giving the girls her recipe box, Beth said, "Keep it. Merry Christmas!" as the girls thanked and hugged her.

The girls said, "We're going to do lots and lots of baking, you'll see!"

Tony walked over to Gabe and shook his hand. The power in Gabe's handshake almost brought Tony to his knees. Tony, rubbing his arm, said, "Thanks for getting here with the bus to get these kids home safe. I can tell they're in safe hands."

"They always were," Gabe replied.

Tony not only missed the sentiment behind Gabe's words but also, not seeing his name tag, which read "Gabrielle."

Tony went to help Beth. She was making lunch bags up for everyone. As they were getting ready to leave, the kids started to give Tony his things back. Tony said, "No WAY, you keep that stuff to remember our adventure." The kids hugged Beth and Tony. As the bus drove away, there was a bright flash, then the bus disappeared.

Meanwhile, back in the police car, the convict was mumbling through his gag. The sergeant said to the other officer, "Pull that gag down."

The convict started ranting and raving. He was in an excited and flustered state. He said to the officers, "Hey, you guys, it was a ghost, I tell you! You guys have to find him!" The convict, even more excited and shaking, said, "He worked me over, but good!"

One officer said "Okay, okay, settle down. We'll get this all figured out."

The convict said, "I can describe him. He wore an old red flannel coat. He had these yellow bootlaces. He tied me up with them. Yeah, yeah, that's it. I'm telling you the truth!"

The police officer put the gag back over his mouth. The sergeant said, "I heard enough of his crazy yacking. What do we do with him? Take him to jail, or the loony bin?"

Then over the police radio, the two officers heard "*gobble, gobble, gobble*." They looked at each other and, at the same time, said, "The loony bin."

At the end of the driveway, Beth looked up and said, "Those northern lights are so beautiful." Beth, Tony, and Frosty paused for a while to stare at the northern lights. Beth said, "What wonderful gifts our Lord gives us."

Heading back to the house arm and arm, Beth rested her head on Tony's shoulder. Tony said, "Beth, I think I'm getting too old for this."

Beth laughed. "You say that every year. I bet if we had a day like today again, you could do it and would love it."

As they got to the entrance of the house, they saw a fresh set of footprints that were not there before. The footprints lead in, but not out.

In front of the door, there were some items. Beth said, "Look, what a beautiful centerpiece." The centerpiece was about two feet tall, made with birch branches, boughs, blossoms, and bows, with colored pinecones, all covered with silver and gold sparkles. Then Beth saw the daily newspaper next to the centerpiece. Beth said, "How did this all get here with this weather?"

Leaning against the door was Tony's rifle. Wrapped around the scope of the rifle was a gold watch. Tony, shocked and confused, said, "What the? It can't be. How did this get here?"

Beth and Tony picked up the items and went into the house. Tony set the rifle back into its gun rack. Looking at it again, Tony said, "I still can't believe this. How did this happen?"

Beth said, "I believe it was your dad."

Tony said, "I believe it also."

Beth said, "I'm going to make us some hot cocoa, then I'll read the newspaper to you. Maybe that will calm us down after the day we had." Beth opened the newspaper and turned pale, turning almost the color of the snow outside.

Tony asked, "Honey, what's wrong?"

Almost going into shock, Beth laid the newspaper down on the table.

After composing herself, Beth began to read the newspaper out loud to Tony. "The last cofounder and co-owner of Little Helpers Outdoor Survival Gear, Randolph [Rudy] Nicholas, has passed away at age ninety-five. It was known that his childhood friends and him went on a field trip and got lost in the woods years ago. They said that experience inspired them to start their company. Their company is credited for saving thousands of people over the years. The company specializes in survival gear and food products of all kinds. Whether you're out at sea, in the desert, or in the mountains, the company carries items for every situation and every need."

Beth and Tony looked at each other and at the same time said, "Could it be?"

☆ THE DAILY NEWS ☆

LAST CO-FOUNDER of "LITTLE HELPER OUTDOOR SURVIVAL GEAR," passes away at age 95

hpany start over **70** years ago. A one room Little Outpost. Little Helpers

Today: The Worldwide Company Giant with fleet of planes, trucks store locations

67

FOUNDERS, DEVELOPERS

Rudy and Donald developing a line of survival gear. Made for extreme outdoor conditions based on a childhood experience. Flashlights, watches with compasses, water purifiers,

Tony and Beth   their dog Frosty

can we
then
rround
trees.
what
bove
the
often
mas
times
tein
bars
Olive
onald
Sam
take
cans

LITTLE HELPER'S CLOTHING LINE

Married for over   50 years, this

cc
W
a
th
s
I
ov
Ch
m
e
th
be
u
n

The article had pictures featuring the company named Little Helpers Outdoor Survival Gear. In one picture was a man named Randolph (Rudy) Nicholas, who was president of the company. He was wearing a necklace with a little red flashlight at the end of it. The article said Rudy referred to it as his lucky charm. Next to Rudy was the vice president, whos' name was Donald. Tony looked closer at the picture. The man was wearing Tony's watch.

The article said these men developed a vast line of compact electronic devises for outdoor use and survival. In another picture was a married couple of fifty-plus years. The man was wearing an old red Bombers hat, and his wife was wearing a familiar scarf. They oversaw the clothing product line for the company. They were said to be the early designers and developers of a vast line of clothing still used today. Tony thought, *Dasher? Vixen?*

Then Beth and Tony looked at another picture. It was of a Middle-Eastern man and two women. They oversaw the food product line for the outdoors and survival line. That product line was beyond imagination.

Some examples were vacuum-sealed meals, jerky, cheeses, candies, nuts, and anything else you could need. Their biggest product was a special line of protein bars. The vacuum sealed label read, "Delicious energy from Beth's kitchen."

Beth looked at Tony and said questionary, "Blitzen, Comet, and Cupid?"

FOOD PRODUCT LINE:

Vacuum sealed, High Protein,
Nutritious and Delicious.
Recipes from Beth's Kitchen
Meats, Cheese, Nuts, Jerky,
Candies, Fruits, Full meal packs

In another picture were two little Asian women. They had a huge line of holiday decorations and centerpieces. They said they remember getting lost with their childhood friends while looking for things to make centerpieces. Then a man they called Nick rescued them. They said the man gave them a radio that was playing Christmas music, which inspired them to make the decorations for the holidays.

Beth pointed at the picture and said, "Tony, there's your radio!"

The article went on to say the women were in charge of the company's charity program. The company name for the charity was called "The Laughing Turkey." The logo for the charity showed a turkey looking over a log at a hunter, with the words "Gobble, gobble, gobble" above the turkey. Every holiday, the charity hand out hundreds of meals to anyone in need.

Beth and Tony said together, "Prancer and Dancer." Along with the meals comes a jar of olives. The label has a picture of a yellow Lab and a Samoyed. Beth and Tony said in awe, "Olive and Frosty?" Beth went over to the centerpiece and took the card off to read it. Beth read, "Dear Beth and Tony, Thanks for everything! Merry Christmas, Love, Your Little Helpers."

Tony questioningly asked Beth, "Are you thinking what I'm thinking?"

Beth answered, "Yes, I think so, like quantum leap!" Trying to absorb what just happened, Beth said, "Come on, it's been quite the day. I have something for you. It was for Christmas, but now's a good time." Beth handed Tony a long-wrapped box.

Tony was grateful but was still thinking about what happened that day. Tony said, "Thanks, honey bunny. Can I guess? Is it that new scope I wanted so bad?"

Beth just sat back, smiled, and watched Tony open the box.

Tony's eyes lit up, and he smiled from ear to ear. It was the best—the nicest camera with a telephoto lens and tripod.

Beth said, "Now you can capture all of nature on film anytime." Tony was like a little kid, excited about all the things he planned to do. Beth said, "Okay, okay, take it easy!"

Beth took Tony by the arm, laid her head on his shoulder, and walked him over to the picture window. They looked out at the herd of deer and the flock of turkeys eating from the feed Tony put out. Beth, Tony, and Frosty just gazed out into the night sky, admiring the stars and the northern lights.

Beth whispered, "LIFE IS GOOD."

About the Authors

Tony and Beth were both born in Wausau, Wisconsin, and lived there to this day. They both worked at Wausau Papers in Brokaw, Wisconsin. That is where they met and fell in love. Tony was blessed with three wonderful children, and Beth was blessed having them as stepchildren.

They've been happily married for more than thirty years. To stay active, they love golfing, traveling, cooking, and, of course, deer hunting.

Their retirement has been quite an adventure so far, and writing this book was one of them.

Printed in the USA
CPSIA information can be obtained
at www.ICGtesting.com
LVHW071248201024
794170LV00015B/108